For Gary Rhodes, with love

–Jim

In memory of Mema

–Jennifer

Sleeping Bear Press™

315 E. Eisenhower Pkwy., Suite 200
Ann Arbor, MI 48108
www.sleepingbearpress.com

Printed and bound in the United States.
10 9 8 7 6 5 4 3 2 1
Library of Congress Cataloging-in-Publication Data
Skofield, James. • Bear and Bird / written by James Skofield ; illustrated by Jennifer Thermes.
pages cm • Summary: "An old bear and a young bird become friends and spend several years together
until the bear's death. The young bird is comforted by memories of their time together"— Provided
by publisher. • ISBN 978-1-58536-835-8 • [1. Friendship—Fiction. 2. Birds—Fiction. 3.
Bears—Fiction. 4. Death—Fiction.] I. Thermes, Jennifer, illustrator. II. Title. •
PZ7.S62835Be 2014 • [E]—dc23 • 2013024896

Bear and Bird

James Skofield ♡ Illustrated by Jennifer Thermes

One spring evening, as Bear walked
through a high meadow toward the woods,
she was stopped by a sound.

A small voice was crying in the tall grass nearby.

"Help," it cried. "Help!"

Bear padded into the tall grass and looked down.
Between her front paws lay Bird. Bird was very
young. He still had patches of downy fluff.
He was trembling.

"I am learning to fly," said Bird,
"but I became dizzy and fell.
Please help me!"

Bear sat down and looked at Bird. She thought for a long time. Then she pushed one big paw forward. Bird flapped his wings and hopped onto her paw. Then he hopped from her paw to her shoulder.

Bear stood and started off again toward the woods. When she reached the edge of the woods, she stopped by a tree and reared onto her hind legs.

She reached one big paw up to a branch. Bird hopped from her shoulder to the branch.

"There," rumbled Bear.
"Now you will be safe."
She dropped back onto all fours
and started off into the woods.

"Thank you!" Bird called after her. "Who are you?"

"I am Bear," grunted Bear and she
disappeared into the woods.

Each day that summer, Bear came to the meadow.
Each day that summer, Bird flew down to greet Bear.
Bird could now fly well. Together, Bear and Bird
looked for berries. Together, they ate them.

Each summer evening, Bird flew into the trees to sleep.
Each summer evening, Bear walked back into the woods.

Summer was ending. Each evening, the sun set earlier.
Each morning was cooler than the one before.
One crisp morning, Bird flew into the woods to meet Bear.

"Do not go into the meadow, Bear!" said Bird.
"I flew over it this morning and saw hunters walking there.
The meadow is not safe for you today."

Bear sat down and thought. "You are right, Bird,"
she grunted. "I will stay hidden in the woods today."

All that day, Bird kept watch.
When the hunters left the meadow, he flew back to Bear.
"The men are gone now," he told her.
"It is safe for you to come out."

"I am glad the men have gone!" grumbled Bear.

Bird was silent. "It is not only the men who must go,"
he chirped softly. "It is time for me to fly south.
I will leave tomorrow."

"Why?" asked Bear. "The days are still warm.
There are still berries to eat."

"Cold weather is coming," said Bird.
"I cannot live through the long, snowy winter.
I must fly somewhere warm."

Bear looked at Bird. Then she turned
and walked off into the woods.
The next morning, Bear felt lonely without Bird.

Soon, freezing rain fell on the meadow.
Bear ate as much as she could.
She grew fat and heavy.
One morning, snow began to fall.
Bear padded deeper into the woods.
She made a den for herself in a warm, dry cave.
Then she curled up and fell asleep.

All winter long, the snows drifted deep.
All winter long, the cold winds blew.
Bear grunted in her sleep. She dreamed of sunshine
and warm berries and the summer meadow.
She dreamed of Bird, too.

Far away in the south,
Bird flew over warm fields.
He pecked at seeds and nuts.
He drank clear water and grew strong.
At night he roosted in trees.
He dreamed of dark, cool woods
and northern hills and berries.
He dreamed of Bear, too.

$\mathcal{T}$he long winter passed.
Snow melted and dripped from trees and rocks.
The air grew softer and warmed the earth.
Bear woke from her winter sleep. She left her den
and walked to the meadow. High above, Bear heard
singing. She looked up and saw Bird.

"Bird!" grunted Bear. "I am happy to see you.
I am glad you came back."

"I am happy to see you, too, Bear," sang Bird.
"I missed you."

For three long summers,
Bear and Bird shared the
meadow. They ate berries.
They drank water.

They drowsed together
in the warm sunshine.

Bird showed Bear where
to find the ripest berries.
Bear showed Bird the secret,
quiet places in the woods.
They were happy.

As their third summer drew to a close, Bear grew stiff.
She could not run as easily as she did before.
She could not see as clearly nor sniff the breeze as keenly.

"What is the matter, Bear?" asked Bird.

"It is nothing," grunted Bear. "I am just old.
I have seen twenty-seven long summers.
I have slept through twenty-seven cold winters.
The sun shines as brightly now as it did when I was younger,
but it does not warm me."

That autumn, Bird stayed with Bear as long as he could.
One cold evening, he knew he must fly south the next day.
He flew down to Bear to say good-bye.
He saw that her paws were trembling.

"I know you must leave, Bird," grunted Bear softly,
"but I wish you did not have to go. I will miss you."

"I will miss you, too, Bear," said Bird.
"But I will fly north again. It is only until spring."

"Yes," said Bear sadly, "only until spring."
Then she slowly walked back into the woods.

Early the next spring, even before all the snow had melted, Bird flew north. He flew to the meadow and perched on a branch.

"Bear!" he sang,

"it is spring! I am back!"

There was no answer.

"Perhaps Bear isn't awake yet," thought Bird.
"After all, it is still very early spring.
I will see her tomorrow."

But Bird did not see Bear the next day.

Or the next. Or the next . . .

The days stretched into weeks
and there was still no sign of Bear.

One rainy morning in late spring,
Bird sat hunched on a dripping tree branch.

He was sad. "I should never have left Bear
last autumn," he thought. "If I had stayed,
we would be together. We would be happy."

Then Bird caught sight of a big, shaggy
animal down at the far end of the meadow.
Bird soared into the air and flew
quickly toward the animal.

"Bear! Bear! Bear!" he sang as he landed on a rock.

The big, shaggy animal turned and looked at Bird. It was a bear. But it was a young bear. It was not Bird's friend. It blinked at Bird.

"Who are you?" the young bear growled.
"Why are you making so much noise?"

"I am Bird," said Bird unhappily.
"I thought you were a friend of mine."

The young bear grunted and sat down on his haunches.
He thought for a long time.

"Oh!" he said. "Now I know who you are.
You were the special friend of my grandmother.
She told me how she rescued you when
you were just a fledgling learning to fly.
She told me she never had a better friend."

"Yes!" cried Bird. "She is my friend. Where is she?"

The bear was silent for a long time.
When he finally answered, his voice was very low.

"Bear went into her den last autumn for the winter sleep.
But she did not come out this spring. She is gone."

Bird let his head droop.
He could not say anything.
The bear looked at him with soft eyes.

"There, now," he rumbled quietly. "You are sad.
But death must come to each of us.
Bear was very old. She had a long, happy life.
You were part of her happiness. You were her friend."

Bird raised his head. "Yes," he croaked.
"I was. But now I am alone. What will I do?"

"Well," said the bear, "my grandmother always
said you knew where to find the best berries.
Why don't you show me?"

Bird sat and thought about Bear.

He thought about her picking him up
from the tall grass when he was very young.
He thought about the summers they shared.
He thought about how stiffly she had moved last autumn.
He thought of her in her winter den.

He remembered her.

Then Bird shook himself all over.
He flew to the young bear's shoulder.
The bear got up and started walking off.

"Are we going the right way?" he grunted.

"A little more to the left," said Bird.
"No, wait. I will fly ahead and show you the way."